# MY FEMINIZATION FANTASY

*An Erotic Crossdressing Short Story!*

By Kate Shulls

**Copyright © All Rights Reserved**

This is a work of fiction. Names, characters, businesses, places, events, locales, and incidents are either the products of the author's imagination or used in a fictitious manner. Any resemblance to actual persons, living or dead, or actual events is purely coincidental.

This book is for adult audiences only. It contains substantial sexually explicit scenes and graphic language which may be considered offensive by some readers. All sexual activity in this work is consensual and all sexually active characters are 18 years of age or older.

Copyright © 2020 Kate Shulls

# Chapter 1

I have been a member of a local association for several years. Since last year I am also increasingly helping the board of the association. Since I already participated in all tasks, I wanted to be an official member of the board. For this, however, I had to convince all eight members. Two were already sold immediately and certainly wanted to support me. Another five were enthusiastic without saying. And one woman was against it. We had already crashed once and she didn't like me. She did, however, always listen to Garrett's opinion. A guy in his late thirties. Just divorced and back single. According to everyone, Michael was charmed by Garrett. I got it; he's definitely a handsome man. I only fear that

Michael is up for it. Because everyone agrees that Garrett is gay and just doesn't dare say it.

I myself have always been curious about sex with a man. I am reasonably convinced that I am at least bi, but I have never done anything like a man. If I were to do something to a man, Garrett would certainly fit the picture to try something with.

Since I see Garrett as the key to Michael and Michael as the key to convincing the rest, I put a lot of energy into getting Garrett on my side. Because he is also not an ugly man, I was not ashamed to do something flirty now and again. During a reception, I was able to chat with him separately for a long time and under the influence of that pint too much, I didn't do a little flirtatious, but I was actually fairly direct. I have suggested fairly clearly that I wanted to provide a return for his support. Unfortunately, he did not want to release anything at the end of the evening.

After a few more weeks, I asked him to eat something in the evening. I finally wanted a final answer and I had said this clearly. He agreed to eat and discuss my candidacy. I had strategically planned the dinner four days before the next board. If I could convince him, he still had enough time to get Michael along, but not enough to change his mind.

We met at Restaurant in our town. Garrett has always been positive lately, so I thought it would be a done deal. I was the first into Restaurant and when Garrett came in, he had a bag from a clothing store. He put it next to him and we started chatting about the cows and calves. The aperitif passed without much excitement, but during the main course, he suddenly said that he would not support me as a candidate, I fired enormously! All options were now off the table. I tried to explain the whole dish to him why he made such a change. In the end, I was pretty desperate. I had been working on this post for a year and a half and wanted to get it.

"What do I have to do to make you change your mind?" I openly asked him.

Garrett suddenly got a smile. With his foot, he pushed the bag that stood with him to my seat. I didn't know what to think.

"If you want me to change my mind," Garrett started, "I want you to go to the bathroom now, take that bag, put on it and put your own things in it."

I could not believe my ears! I looked briefly at the bag and saw that it was one from the Hunkemöller.

"If you don't do this, you can write your chance of a board position on your stomach," he said with a nasty smile.

I doubted. What was in that bag? Did he mean his threat? Can I walk through the Restaurant with a bag like that from the Hunkemöller?

Garrett kept looking at me, amused. I decided to just go to the toilet. Then I could just think there for ease. I also wanted to go confident. Then maybe I could read a reaction from Garrett's face.

I picked up the bag and stood up without saying much. I looked Garrett in the eye. He kept staring at me. Yet I noticed a hint of relief. Had he played poker and bluffed?

I walked to the toilet and chose the rear toilet. I quickly checked to see if there was anyone else, but I was alone.
Once in the toilet, I looked at what I had been given. There were three things in it: a black ladies' thong and tights with an open crotch and plenty of makeup.

Again, that doubt. I wanted to try something with a man for a long time. I have been secretly horny on Ladies Lingerie for ages and I had already bought and put on a pair of tights with makeup and a wig while masturbating on several occasions. And I had a submissive side, craving to be dominated. Even my bottom was naturally rather wide and perky, fitting for sexy lingerie. But that was all completely private. No one was aware of that. If I agreed, I would expose a lot of myself. On the other hand, he did that too. So I think I could count on discretion. The consequences are that I get a position in the association, that I will have sex and that I can do several fetishes.

I decide to risk it. I change my clothes. The string is replacing my boxer shorts. This also appears to have an open cross. I can already feel the excitement, especially when I put on the tights. This has a print from the toe to the top. Since I was no longer allowed to put on my socks, this means that the pantyhose would be somewhat visible when I sit down. Then my pants crawl up a little and everyone can see my ankle.

I'm going back to Garrett. I feel my dick (which hangs freely) getting stiff. When I sit down, I give him the bag. When he looks into it, I see him smile broadly.

"I just ordered dessert for us. I hope that's okay?" However, is everything he says? So I have to sit still.

Furthermore, it is about cows and calves.

After dessert, we pay and go outside.

"Let's have another drink at my house. I still live nearby. "He said. Now it's going to happen, I think.

Once he has arrived, he pours in a drink. He turned the bag over on the living room table and said, "You have already proven that you have taken off your own clothes, but not yet that you are wearing the others. I want you to take off all your clothes and show me what you are wearing."

The game had really started.

I take off my sweater and t-shirt. Garrett is now sitting in his seat.

After I have also taken off my shoes and pants, I am standing in only the tights and thong for him. My stiff dick stands proudly through the opening.

"Come here and take it easy."

I stand between his legs and start to spin slowly so that he can look well. When I put my ass to him, I pull the pantyhose up a little extra so that my ass goes up and down with the pantyhose. I hear him smile approvingly.
As soon as I am completely turned around, I stop facing him. My dick sticks out to him. Garrett stretches his arm to grab my dick. But I won't allow this yet. I grasp his wrist with one hand and briefly take control. Now I want to make sure I get what I want out of it. And that takes effort because I am now horny.

"Tut-tutut," I say while I put the finger on his lips to stop his protest. "If you want to continue, Garrett, I want my post on the board."

Garrett nods, that is already inside. However, I am not ready yet. I take my finger off his lips and let his wrist down. I lean on the backrest of the seat, stretch my legs and warp my back. After spinning, I had seen a mirror behind me and Garrett could see my ass tightly in it. As I brought my face straight in front of his, I also saw that he was looking at it. Man, this was exciting! Being lifted like this by someone else.

I looked him in the eye, his face a few centimetres from mine "I don't just want the function. Within this and a few months, you will become my biggest fan, you support my ideas and you help convince others."

"And what do I get?" He asked, doubtfully.

"Then I will become your private hooker to participate the way you want sir."

Without waiting for a reaction, I sink my knees; I skilfully open his pants and take out his dick. I've never done this before, but don't hesitate. With one hand I start to knead his balls and at the same time, I start to blow him.
It's the first time I taste a dick. The taste is not bad at all. I hear Garrett sigh and moan happily.

While I am on my knees, I make sure that my butt is still tight and my back stays curved to give him the best view.

Soon I taste his pre-cum and while I vigorously suck on his glans and suck, I hear his breathing speed up. His moans get louder and then he sprays and he keeps spraying. As an accomplished whore, I try to swallow everything, but due to the large amount, this doesn't work. I think he hasn't finished in a few months.

I let him recover from the orgasm and look at him. If he is a bit more positive, I smile broadly at him and he at me. Good as I am, I bend back and begin to lick his dick, now covered in sperm, clean. When his dick is clean, I sit back like a good schoolgirl. I sit on my knees in front of him, butt on my heels and back straight.

I look at him with a smile and lick the last seed off my fingers and hands.

"That was delicious and a horny show." Said Garrett.

"Unfortunately, I have to go now, Garrett," I said in my sweetest voice. I also try to sound as submissive as possible to give some power back. "Just think about my proposal." I end with a wink. I put my clothes on the lingerie I got from Garrett. This one is mine now, I think and I am leaving before he can do anything else.

# Chapter 2

I no longer hear from Garrett. But a few days later, I get a call from another board member that my application has been accepted. Did mission accomplish?

If I thought the cold was doing the dishes, I would be disappointed. Just two hours after the phone call, I received a text from Garrett:

"Hooker, prepare yourself tomorrow, 19:00, my apartment. You know where." Wow, the tone was set and after the experience earlier this week, I immediately got horny again. I started wondering what would he do to me this time, previously it was merely a blowjob. His way of doing things was also enormously exciting.

The next day I was at his door nicely on time. He let me into the building via the bell. However, even before I reached his door, I received another text message.

"Undressing in the hallway and coming in naked."

Here we go again. I am standing in the hallway at his door. Several apartments open onto the corridor. But I dare it. I already said it was time to say b.

I ring the bell. It seems to take forever for Garrett to open the door. And I thought I'd been caught sixteen times.
Garrett smiles approvingly when he sees me standing naked.

"Good hooker, come on in." Again appealing to him: hooker. I really feel less. And I'm getting more excited.

I follow Garrett into the living room. He sits down in the seat where he sat last time. He is also still wearing his clothes. I myself wait for his instructions on what to do.

He spreads his legs and gives a sign that I have to sit back in between. I do as indicated. I sit on my knees between his legs. My dick rises proudly between my legs.

"Hooker, you are now appointed, so it's time to start your part of the appointment," says Garrett van de Waal. "You are my hooker now. You do what I want when I want, how I want and where I want. If I send you a message, I expect a response within 15 minutes. If you don't stick to this, everyone will soon know what kind of slut you are."

Clearly; I have to listen.

Like a lamb, I respond, "yes, Garrett. I will listen."

He laughs again, approvingly.

"Stand up and let me see what you have."

I stand up and show him my body. He also stands straight and turns around me and looks at me from head to toe. He also starts to feel everywhere. I feel his hands on my body, on my chest, on my buttocks. Standing behind me, he grabs my dick and starts to jerk me off. This feels incredibly nice and I can't help but moan.

"If you behave, I will also reward you from time to time, the whore of mine." He whispers in my ear.

"This is so delicious and I do what you want;" Was all I could release.

"Very well," Garrett said.

He lets go of dick and slaps my ass with the flat hand.

The chat surprises me, but it feels nice.

He hits again. Again so hard and again I like it.

He keeps beating me and with every slap, I moan louder and louder. My breathing also becomes faster and heavier.

Then he directs me to the seat. I have to sit on my knees on the couch with my butt up. I know what's coming next, but still, get nervous. As horny as I am, I have never done this before.

I feel his hands go over my ass. With one finger he starts massaging my asterisk. This already feels nice and I start to relax.

Then I hear how his pants fall to the floor. I look around and see him standing there with his stiff dick, ready to fuck me like the whore that I am.

Apparently, he had prepared everything today because he suddenly has lubricant on his hands and rubs his dick and my ass with it.

"Come on, fuck me!" I tell him.

He places his glans against my ass and gently pushes on. I try to relax and suddenly he pushes on. His dick suddenly shoots my ass.

I moaned loudly. This feels nice. I am completely filled and then he starts to bump. First quietly to let me get used to it, but I notice that he wants it harder. Oh yes, I am the hooker and I will certainly behave like that.
I release all the brakes and moan loudly while enjoying!

"Oooh, fuck me! Fuck your whore! Let me feel that pole of yours! Harder! HARDER!"

Garrett is increasing the pace and is going faster and faster. We both enjoy it. And then I suddenly feel his hot cum squirting in my ass.

Exhausted, Garrett falls into the seat next to me.

After some recovery, Garrett takes my still hard cock and starts to jerk me off. This feels great.

It doesn't leave him unmoved either because I see how his dick gets stiff again. While he still jerks me off, I bend over and start to blow him. I suck his dick back completely stiff. Once this is successful, I turn around and sit on his dick. His dick slips easily through my pipe and the seed that was still inside me. I'm starting to ride him. In the meantime, he grabs my dick and starts to jerk me off. Together we work towards an orgasm.

I can't hold it anymore and squirt my load loudly. Because of this, my ass squeezes itself together and this also drives Garrett over the edge. For the second time, he sprays my ass full.

Now we are both completely exhausted. After recovering, Garrett says I can go. I have to go to the street with that full butt. Now I really feel like a whore.

At the door, Garrett tells me to keep an eye on my cell phone.

Will undoubtedly be prosecuted.

There have been a few months since that first night that I have sucked Garrett and we still have sex regularly. With his help, I am the rising star in our association and so I continue to play the whore for him. Although I have to be honest, I also enjoy it to the full. So I think I would continue even without him support me anymore.

We have done a lot together in those few months. At the very beginning, he put me on my knees again and asked what was possible. I then said that just about everything was on the table.

Very often Garrett lets me show up in a beautiful blonde wig, makeup, Women lingerie, nylons Winden on him and I think it's super horny to wear them, so that works out nicely. Occasionally I put on sexy nylons at home to surprise him. Then I can also enjoy the smooth fabric on my legs for longer. Usually, when I do this, I sit on his dick within five minutes to fuck him.

Fortunately, Garrett has a high recovery so that he can cum several times. My visits to Garrett often last for many hours and he fucks me completely dull.

He recently let me come by and tied me to his living room table with a set of nylons. He had tied me up so that I could see the television well. On this, he played porn of sissy men all afternoon while I was tied up. He himself was busy in the house and in between he fucked me hard and long. When he wasn't fucking me himself, he put a vibrator in my ass and put it in full. Because of this treatment and the many horny films with submissive sissies getting fucked, I came six times that afternoon! The last time there was not even any more seed. I was that empty! When he was finally fed up with me, he released me, but before I could leave, I had to lick my sperm off the ground. I found this so humiliating! But at the same time, very horny again.

Garrett, clearly understood very well that I was keen on that submission and the humiliating. He never spoke to me by name. I was always his whore or slut or whatever. Sometimes he also let me come by and fucked me for five minutes and then threw me outside again. I was just another sex toy to play with whenever he liked it. I felt more feminine by the day and I simply loved it!

A few weeks ago, I received another text from Garrett that I had to come by. He wanted sex. Unfortunately, at that time, I was on the weekend with friends and it was, therefore, impossible to give in to his demands. This was the first time this happened. Garrett was not set up with this:

"This is not the appointment slut! If I want to get into your slut cunt, it should be available here!"

"I'm sorry, honey, but let's go eat something on Monday and I'll make it up. Promised. Good things come to those who wait ;-)" I sent back.

"On Monday my brother comes to sleep with his family, so that is not possible."

"Then we eat and see later in the week. And who knows what happens :-)"

I knew what I wanted to make happen. And that plan had two sides. He once told me he was fantasizing about having sex in public, somewhere in an alley or something. I could take care of that.

I also noticed that he was always hotter when he had me put on lingerie. He also increasingly set up porn with curvy sissies getting feminized and fucked. Men who looked just like woman. I suspect that he also wanted to do that.

I had already secretly bought some rugs. I had been working my bottom ever since the first couple of meetings. In addition, I had also bought a pair of stilettos (and practiced a lot at home). Finally, I had bought a blonde wig and found someone who wanted to help me perfect my make up.

On Monday, I had a day off and took ample time to prepare myself. Extensive showering, everything shaved well and my outfit was chosen for the evening: a tight rose dress, dark nylons with a motif and suspenders, black stilettos and a black lace lingerie set. The panties were provided with an open butt, which made it easier for Garrett to reach.

I first went to an acquaintance that would help me with my makeup. I completely changed. She also gave me a couple of fake breasts so that I would be a great woman. After being painted, I looked in the mirror and saw a horny woman who was ready to fuck well.

While I was walking through the city, I felt very fiercely viewed. Several men even imitated me. This did increase my self-confidence.

I was the first at the Restaurant so I could put myself in such a way that I had a view of the room and could see Garrett coming.

I quickly sent him a WhatsApp "I'm already there and I have a surprise for you ;-)"

He arrived about five minutes later. When the waitress brought him, I saw him looking doubtful (but also hopeful). I stood up to kiss him.

"Hey Garrett, you are still coming," I said with a wink.

Garrett's eyes fell out of his sockets. I subtly turned around to move my chair so that it had a nice view of my back.

"Surprised?" I asked naughtily when we were both seated.

"Whole," he stammered. He was completely lost.

"Do you like it?" I asked.

"Very beautiful!"

"Do you find it sexy?"

He then picked up again. We were secluded in the Restaurant and could talk fairly freely.

"Slut, you look great and I want to take you from now and here on the table."

I had taken off one of my shoes under the table and now I put my stocking foot on his crotch. His erection was clearly felt. In the meantime, I looked at him as horny as possible.

"Aren't you glad you waited for something?"

"I am very happy, but I am sorry that I have to wait so long before I can do something with it."

At this moment, the menu came and we had to focus on the food. The dinner itself went smoothly. I regularly rubbed my feet along his legs to his dick. That's how I kept it stiff and horny. Halfway through, I also decided to go to the bathroom. When I walked past him, he stopped me for a moment and let his hand glide up my leg and grabbed my dick under my skirt.

At the toilets, I had to be careful that I did not enter the men's room.

After dinner, we walked towards my car together. As a gentleman, he wasn't going to let me go alone. As soon as we were out on the street, he put his arm around me and subtly lowered his hand to my butt.

"I'm looking forward to you so much. He whispered in my ear.

A little further, we turned into an alley. I had come here before to see if there were cameras or something like that.

Halfway down the alley was another porch with a railing in front. I pushed Garrett with his back against the wall
"What are you doing?" He asked startled.

"Ssst, surprise. I said with a wink.

I squatted and quickly opened his pants. His stiff dick jumped out of my underpants towards my face! I quickly grabbed his jerk and started to blow it too deep as he likes it.

After a few minutes, Garrett straightened me and turned around, so I leaned over the railing. Because of this, I hung my upper body in the alley and I was visible to everyone, but I didn't care. I was Garrett, a horny whore and that's how I behaved.

While Garrett pulled up my skirt, I encouraged him to fuck me!

"Oooh grab me! Fuck my whore! Squirt my slut cunt!"

Garrett hit me on the ass, which made me even hotter. I looked over my shoulder at him and looked at him in a whorey way.

"Do you want my dick whore?" He asked.

Even before I could answer, he pushed his dick in my ass all at once. I moaned the entire street together.

Garrett started to fuck me hard and deep and hit my ass.

"Here! You like this! Being taken like a slut. Feel my dick in your slut cunt!"

I was completely crazy about horniness! And moaned loudly and kept talking to him in a whorey voice. He gave no mercy and his thrusts became harder each time to a moment where I suddenly felt his dick swelling deep inside of me and I heard him shouting into me.

After this fucking party we settled ourselves a bit, I licked his dick clean and then I pulled my skirt back and walked on.

While walking, I felt how Garrett ran his cum out of my ass and it came down my stockings.

I felt like a real slut as I walked there.

We said goodbye to the car.

"See you next time." Garrett said with a wink as he gave my ass one last spank.

33

The End.

www.ingramcontent.com/pod-product-compliance
Lightning Source LLC
Chambersburg PA
CBHW021407160726
47994CB00007B/3117